DANNY McGEE
DRINKS THE SEA

ANDY STANTON & NEAL LAYTON

schwartz & wade books · new york

Text copyright © 2016 by Andy Stanton

Jacket art and interior illustrations copyright © 2016 by Neal Layton

Visit us on the Web! randomhousekids.com

Educators and librarians, for a variety of teaching tools, visit us at RHTeachersLibrarians.com

Library of Congress Cataloging-in-Publication Data

Names: Stanton, Andy. | Layton, Neal, illustrator.

Title: Danny McGee drinks the sea / by Andy Stanton ; illustrated by Neal Layton.

Description: First American edition. | New York : Schwartz & Wade Books, 2017.

Originally published by Hodder Children's Books, London, in 2016.

Summary: When Danny's sister doubts his boast that he can drink the
entire sea, he not only proves he was right, he swallows everything else in sight.

Identifiers: LCCN 2016025799 (print) | LCCN 2016053902 (ebook)

ISBN 978-1-5247-1736-0 (hardback) | ISBN 978-1-5247-1737-7 (glb)

ISBN 978-1-5247-1738-4 (ebook) | ISBN 978-1-5247-1738-4 (ebk)

Subjects: | CYAC: Stories in rhyme. | Brothers and sisters—Fiction.

Humorous stories. | Tall tales. | BISAC: JUVENILE FICTION / Humorous

Stories. | JUVENILE FICTION / Family / Siblings.

Classification: LCC PZ8.3.S7879 Dan 2017 (print) | LCC PZ8.3.S7879 (ebook) | DDC [E]—dc23

The text of this book is set in StampGothic.

The illustrations were rendered in mixed media.

MANUFACTURED IN CHINA

2 4 6 8 10 9 7 5 3 1

First American Edition

One summer's day, Danny and Frannie McGee hopped into a car and drove down to the sea.

The sea was all sparkly,
blue as can be.

"I bet I can drink it,"
said Danny McGee.

Said Frannie, "No, Danny,
I cannot agree.
You'll **never** drink all of it,
Danny McGee."

"I will, just you watch,"
replied Danny McGee.
"Please fetch me a straw
and then you will see."

So Fran fetched a straw that was longer than she.

And Danny McGee started drinking the sea.

In ten minutes' time
there was no sea to see,

because all of the sea
was in Danny McGee.

"I cannot believe it,"
said Frannie McGee.
"You've drunk the whole thing.
It's **AMAZING** to me!"

"I'm **just getting started**,"
said Danny McGee.

And he flicked out his tongue
and he swallowed a **tree**.

And he swallowed a **bird**

and he swallowed a **bee.**

And he swallowed a **cat**
who was drinking some tea.

And he swallowed a fly

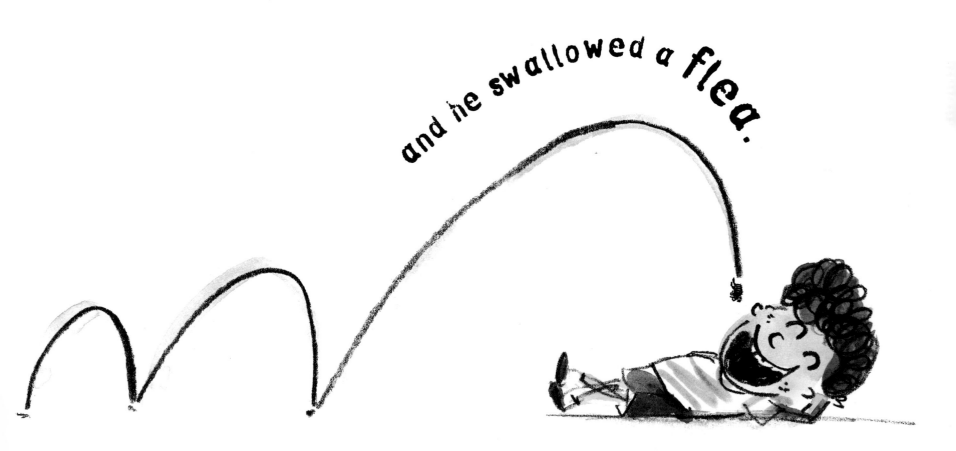

and he swallowed a flea.

And he swallowed a **man**
who was learning to ski.

And he swallowed a **pie**
and he swallowed a pea.

And he swallowed the weather girl
on the **TV**.

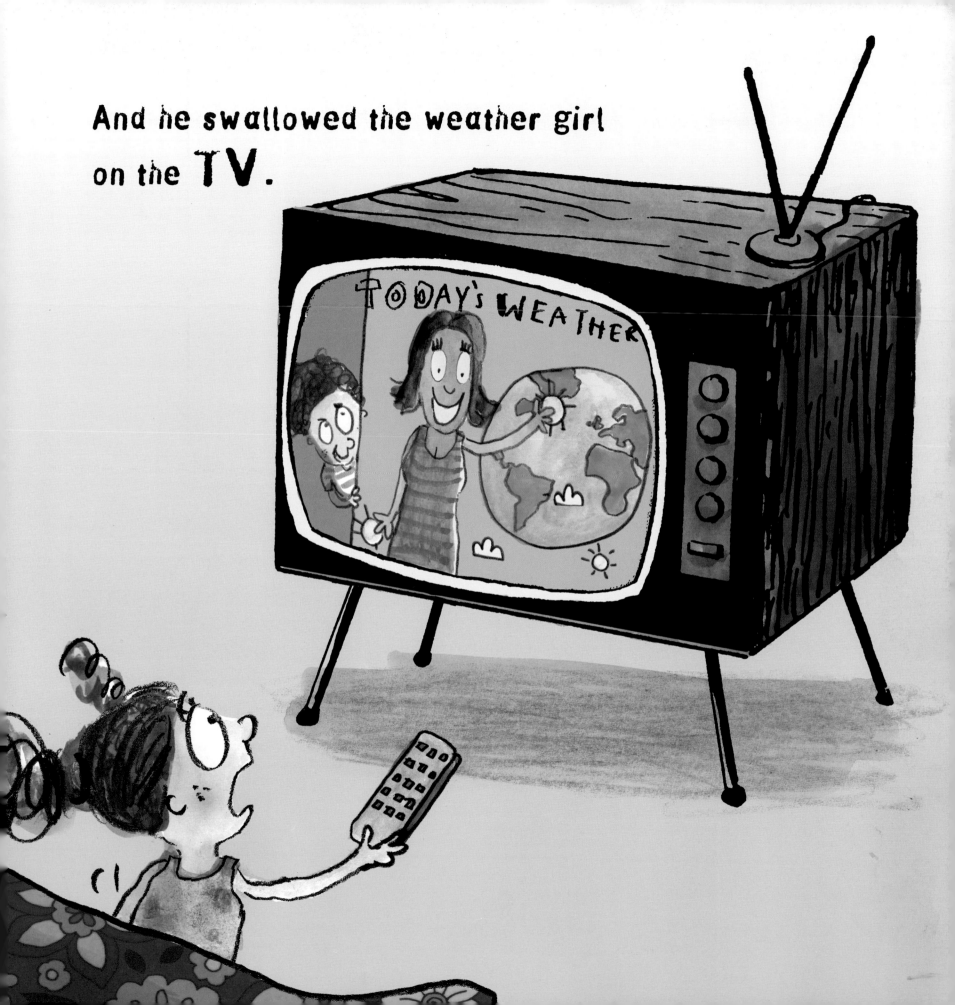

"You're naughty!" said Frannie.
"I'm telling, you'll see!"
But Danny just giggled . . .

and swallowed a **swee.**

And I know that you think there's
no such thing as a swee,
but believe me, there **was**,
before Danny McGee.

S is for "Swee"

The Swee is a hairy
sort of fellow na ive
the upper flower easte
regions of the Wester
Northlands of the
South. Little is known
about these remarkable an
except that y

"I will swallow it all!"
shouted Danny McGee.
And he swallowed the sand
where the sea used to be.

And he swallowed
the **mountains,**
and every last **tree.**

And he swallowed the jungles.

He did it with glee.

And he swallowed the people
and that includes **me**.
And I'm writing this book
inside Danny McGee.

And he swallowed America,
land of the free.

And he swallowed up London,
chim chim cher-ee!

And he swallowed the alphabet **A, B,** and **C.**

And he swallowed the numbers **1, 2,** and **3.**

And he swallowed until
there was no more to see.

said Danny McGee.

But then Frannie said . . .

"Danny, you didn't get me."

And she opened her mouth
and **s w a l l o w e d**

Danny McGee.

"Little brothers can be **SO** annoying sometimes."